I Had a Hippopotamus

Hector Viveros Lee

Lee & Low Books Inc. · New York

For my parents,
whose roots gave me wings.

Printed in Hong Kong by South China Printing Co. (1988) Ltd.

Book design by Tania Garcia
Book production by The Kids at Our House

The text is set in Antikva Margaret
The illustrations are rendered using gouache, India ink, and watercolor by the following process: First, white
gouache is applied to illustration board with pencil drawings. After the paint dries, black India ink is brushed
quickly over the entire surface, saturating only the penciled areas. Once the ink is dry, the board is washed off,
leaving a simulated woodcut drawing. The image is then transferred to acetate and also onto a clean illustration
board, where it is painted with watercolor and gouache. The acetate film is then placed over the painting,
creating a cross between a woodcut and a stained-glass window.

10 9 8 7 6 5 4 3 2 1
First Edition

Library of Congress Cataloging-in-Publication Data
Lee, Hector Viveros
I had a hippopotamus/by Hector Viveros Lee.—1st ed.
p. cm.
Summary: An imaginative boy opens a box of animal crackers and gives his family
members a hippopotamus, anaconda, rhinoceros, and other exotic animals.
ISBN 1-880000-62-8 (paperback)
(1. Animals—Fiction. 2. Imagination—Fiction.) I. Title.
PZ7.L512465Iaad 1996   95-21730
(E)—dc20   CIP   AC

I had a hippopotamus.

But I gave it to my mom.

I had an anaconda.

But I gave it to my dad.

I had a rhinoceros.

But I gave it to my sister.

I had an elephant.

But I gave it to my baby brother.

I had a kangaroo.

But I gave it to my grandma.

I had a pangolin.

But I gave it to my grandpa.

I had a coyote.

But I gave it to my uncle.

I had a marabou.

But I gave it to my cousin.

I had a jaguar.

But I gave it to my best friend.

I had an orangutan.

But I gave it to my neighbor.

I had a wart hog.

But I gave it to the girl next door.

I had a crocodile.

But I gave it to my teacher.

I had a small, scampering,

sly, naughty, loveable

kitten.

And I kept it for myself.